S0-BGF-595

EXPL🧭RER
ACADEMY

FIELD JOURNAL

NATIONAL
GEOGRAPHIC

WASHINGTON, D.C.

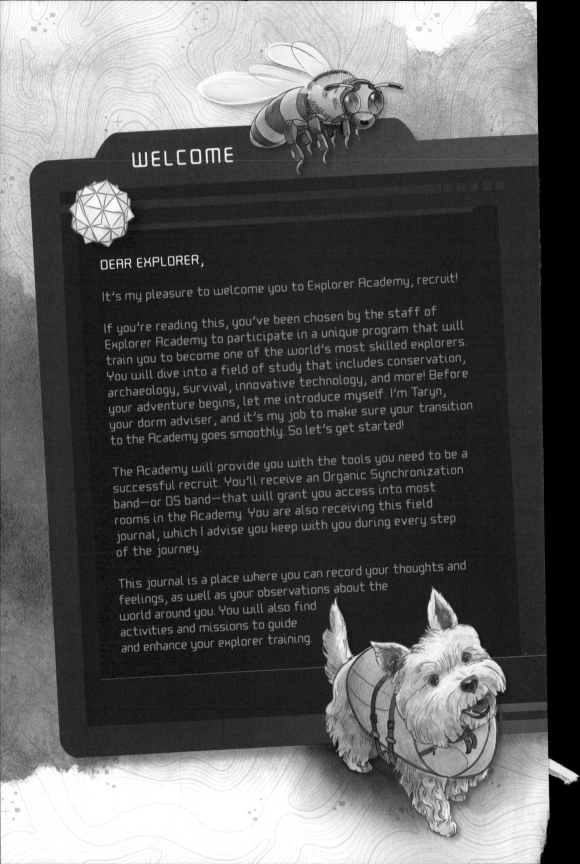

WELCOME

DEAR EXPLORER,

It's my pleasure to welcome you to Explorer Academy, recruit!

If you're reading this, you've been chosen by the staff of Explorer Academy to participate in a unique program that will train you to become one of the world's most skilled explorers. You will dive into a field of study that includes conservation, archaeology, survival, innovative technology, and more! Before your adventure begins, let me introduce myself. I'm Taryn, your dorm adviser, and it's my job to make sure your transition to the Academy goes smoothly. So let's get started!

The Academy will provide you with the tools you need to be a successful recruit. You'll receive an Organic Synchronization band—or OS band—that will grant you access into most rooms in the Academy. You are also receiving this field journal, which I advise you keep with you during every step of the journey.

This journal is a place where you can record your thoughts and feelings, as well as your observations about the world around you. You will also find activities and missions to guide and enhance your explorer training.

Remember, this journal is about you! Work your way through it from beginning to end, or flip through it and see what interests you. Your fellow recruits all have different ways of approaching it. Cruz Coronado loves to complete the missions. Emmett Lu enjoys tackling the activities. And Bryndis Jónsdóttir likes answering the question prompts. How you do it is up to you!

Enjoy your new adventure, recruit! And if you ever need any help, come see me at the front desk. I'll be happy to answer your questions, and Hubbard always looks forward to being scratched behind the ears.

Good luck, and dare to explore!

TARYN SECLIFF
DORM ADVISER

RECRUIT INTAKE FORM

NAME

AGE   COUNTRY

FAVORITE ACTIVITIES

SPECIAL SKILLS

EXPLORATION

Which field of exploration are you most interested in? Circle one or more.

- animal biology
- anthropology
- archaeology
- artificial intelligence
- astronomy
- cryptology
- engineering
- oceanography
- survival training

COURSE SELECTION

Select five courses to take while you're at the Academy.

- basic Mandarin
- cartography
- codes and ciphers
- computer coding
- deep-sea diving
- desert survival
- Egyptology
- explorer history
- meteorology
- mysteries of the Aztec
- ocean biology
- principles of flight
- robotics
- rock climbing

WHAT MADE YOU INTERESTED IN THE FIELDS OF EXPLORATION AND COURSES YOU CHOSE?

_____

_____

_____

_____

_____

_____

_____

_____

_____

_____

_____

_____

_____

_____

_____

_____

_____

_____

_____

_____

_____

_____

_____

_____

_____

_____

DATE / TIME ::   LOCATION ::

SUBJECT ::

These free pages are for you to write about anything on your mind. Continue answering a prompt or doodle what your own tech inventions will look like. Explorers love being creative, so go ahead and start writing!

DATE / TIME ::

LOCATION ::

SUBJECT ::

EA explorers are conservationists, meaning they protect and preserve the environment. Your missions will often involve learning how to track, observe, identify, and record different animals and their behavior. This crucial information may one day help prevent the extinction of species.

BACKYARD BEHAVIOR

MISSION 1.0

YOUR MISSION, SHOULD YOU CHOOSE TO ACCEPT IT, is to observe the animals in your environment. Go outside to the closest outdoor spot and write down the name of any wildlife you see, where you found it, what it was doing, and the date. Don't see any? Look closer. Are there ants? Ladybugs? Wildlife is everywhere if you know where to look for it.

MISSION 1.0 | MISSION 2.0 | MISSION 3.0 | MISSION 4.0 | MISSION 5.0

DRAW A PICTURE OF WHAT YOU FOUND HERE.

AROUND THE WORLD

You and your fellow Explorer Academy recruits will travel all over the world aboard a ship called *Orion*. If you could explore any five places in the world, where would you go? Why?

1

2

3

4

5

If you could design your own ship, what name would you give it?

DATE / TIME ::　　　　　　　　LOCATION ::

SUBJECT ::

WHAT'S YOUR MOOD?

Emmett engineered himself a pair of high-tech "emoto-glasses" that change color and shape with his mood. Yellow frames mean he's happy, and circular frames with pink dots and turquoise streaks mean he's excited. But those are just a few of the different colors and shapes they display. If you had your own pair of emoto-glasses, what colors and shapes would yours turn and what moods would they convey?

DRAW AND COLOR THE KEY USED TO DECODE YOUR GLASSES BELOW!

SHAPE	COLOR	EMOTION

NOW TRY DRAWING YOUR OWN PAIR OF EMOTO-GLASSES!

Add a little thought from Emmett here!

DATE / TIME ::

LOCATION ::

SUBJECT ::

BOOKS THAT STICK WITH YOU

Books can take you on a journey without leaving your seat—and they can inspire you to explore places you've never been. Cruz's mother left him a clue in a book full of adventure and excitement that the two of them read together over and over: *The Lion, the Witch and the Wardrobe* by C. S. Lewis. Have you ever read a book that you loved so much that you read it more than once? What is it about that book that makes it special? Did it make you want to discover a new place and meet new people?

FAVORITE BOOK

WHY

FAVORITE PART

DATE / TIME ::   LOCATION ::

SUBJECT ::

PICK YOUR TEAM

Explorer teams need to support each other, think on their toes, and be brave enough to face dangerous situations. If you could pick five of your friends to be on your explorer training team, who would you choose? Choose carefully—the success of your next mission could depend on it!

Now name your team after a famous explorer:

TRY DRAWING PICTURES OF YOUR TEAMMATES.

DATE / TIME ::

LOCATION ::   22.0964° N   I   159.5261° W

SUBJECT ::

DATE / TIME ::

LOCATION ::

SUBJECT ::

What's one of the most important tools a recruit needs before embarking on a mission? Information! And one of the best places to explore a topic is at a library. The Explorer Academy library contains a vast maze of bookshelves, but you can use your local or school library for this assignment.

LIBRARY DEEP DIVE

MISSION 2.0

YOUR MISSION, RECRUIT: Sharpen your research skills by exploring your library. Search for books in each of the categories on the list. For extra credit, choose the book that interests you most and check it out.

mission 1.0 | **MISSION 2.0** | mission 3.0 | mission 4.0 | mission 5.0

FIND A BOOK FROM EACH CATEGORY AND WRITE DOWN THE TITLE AND AUTHOR.

A biography or autobiography of an explorer:

A map atlas of the world:

A nonfiction book about butterflies:

A biography or autobiography of an inventor:

A book about codes and ciphers:

A biography or autobiography of an astronomer:

A book about endangered animals:

A tourist guide to any country in the world:

A book about hiking or mountain climbing:

A book about predicting weather:

DATE / TIME ::   LOCATION ::

SUBJECT ::

GET PACKING

Listen up, explorer! You are being sent on an official mission to the Namib Desert. Look up what the weather is this time of year and pick five things to pack. The items you choose are critical to your survival.

DATE / TIME ::

LOCATION ::

SUBJECT ::

EXPLORER TIPS AND TRICKS FROM THE FIELD:
PREPARING FOR SUCCESS

ERIKA BERGMAN

Erika Bergman
Explorer & Engineer

Expert engineer and deep-sea submersible pilot Erika Bergman weaves her way through unique underwater ecosystems few people have ever seen. Bergman has come across problems that interfere with missions—like heavy storms in Papua New Guinea, an island nation in the southwestern Pacific Ocean, that forced her to keep changing locations and target new dive spots. Luckily, she was able to wait out the storm and keep herself entertained by playing Ping-Pong with the crew. Even though no mission runs entirely smoothly, preparation is key for success.

This underwater adventurer believes mental and physical preparation are essential for fieldwork. Before she begins fieldwork, she often takes a full 24 hours to be by herself, filling her day by walking, writing, and prepping with thought games.

Take a page from Bergman's notes and write—this journal is a great place to jot down reflections before an expedition! But nothing really gets you in the right mind-set more than packing your bag. Bergman finds that by prepping her gear, she is able to mentally prepare for her upcoming trip.

After all that careful planning, it's time to get out there! Bergman urges young adventurers to "allow their curiosity to guide them. It's easy to 'wonder' about the world and stay put, but an explorer is a person who wonders and then wanders!" Just remember to always tell someone where you're going, and to pack your GPS unit and some sturdy shoes before heading out.

What would you be most excited to discover on a deep-sea expedition?

_____

_____

_____

_____

_____

_____

_____

_____

_____

_____

_____

_____

_____

_____

_____

_____

_____

_____

_____

_____

_____

_____

Erika's a deep-sea submersible pilot!

DATE / TIME ::

LOCATION ::

SUBJECT ::

DESIGN A DRONE

Cruz has a tiny drone named Mell that looks like a honeybee—the perfect disguise for a micro air vehicle that can help you get out of a sticky situation! If you had your own miniature drone, what would it look like? Draw it here and give it a name.

Add a little thought
from Mell here!

DATE / TIME ::

LOCATION ::

SUBJECT ::

GET MOVING

Recruits have to be ready to spring into action at any moment, which is why physical training is important. Growing up in Hawaii, Cruz became an avid surfer. What is your favorite activity to do outdoors? How do you feel when you are doing it?

WHAT OUTDOOR SPORT WOULD YOU LIKE TO TRY? WHY?

DAVID GRUBER

David Gruber
Marine Biologist & Ocean Explorer

Some explorers discovered what they wanted to do by learning about it in a classroom. Some thought about many different paths before choosing the one that worked for them. And still others, like marine biologist and ocean explorer David Gruber, found what they loved by getting outside. Just like Cruz, Gruber connected with the world around him by riding the waves, and he believes surfing helped him with his work. "I view each expedition like an ever changing wave: It may wash out, toss me around like a rag doll, or provide an epic and unforgettable tube ride."

You many not know what you want to pursue right away, and that's okay. If you take risks and explore lots of things, you'll be sure to find the right fit that makes you happy. From photography to engineering to conservation, or something completely unique, there are a lot of options out there. The next step? "Stay curious and always ask questions—even if they seem super silly." The best recruits at the Academy aren't afraid to make mistakes or to not know something. Asking for help and getting a little guidance is all part of the training to become a top-notch explorer.

Self-doubt can sometimes also be a part of your training, even when you're going after your goals. Gruber advises that you should never doubt yourself too much, and that following your interests is always worthwhile: "We are all born 'explorers'! It is a part of your DNA. And don't let anyone tell you otherwise!"

What kinds of exploration do you want to try? Archaeology? Journalism? Mountaineering?

DATE / TIME ::

LOCATION ::

SUBJECT ::

DATE / TIME ::

LOCATION ::

SUBJECT ::

SIMPLE CIPHER

Sometimes, Explorer Academy recruits need to use coded messages to keep sensitive information out of enemy hands. One of the simplest ways to write a coded message is to use a reverse alphabet cipher. Write out the alphabet A–Z in one column, and next to it write out the alphabet from Z–A. So A=Z, B=Y, C=X, etc. Using this code, the word ALPHABET is spelled ZOKSZYVG!

A	Z

WRITE A MESSAGE USING THIS CIPHER. THEN COPY THE KEY FOR ANOTHER RECRUIT TO DECODE YOUR MESSAGE.

_____
_____
_____
_____
_____
_____
_____
_____

What do you think Lani would
write in her coded message?

DATE / TIME ::

LOCATION ::

SUBJECT ::

DATE / TIME ::

LOCATION ::

SUBJECT ::

When you are sent to a new location, you'll need to quickly immerse yourself in your surroundings—the nature, the people, the history, and the culture. Let's practice with a place you're familiar with first.

EXPLORE NEXT DOOR

MISSION 3.0

YOUR MISSION, RECRUIT: Find the answers to these questions about the place where you live. Start by observing your surroundings, and get more information at your local library or historical society, by talking to family and friends, or by searching online.

MISSION 1.0 | MISSION 2.0 | **MISSION 3.0** | MISSION 4.0 | MISSION 5.0

What is the geography of your town? Are you in the mountains, a desert, or a city? Are you near water?

What kinds of plants and animals can you find where you live?

Who is the most famous person to have lived in your town?

What is the oldest building in your town?

What event in your town brings the most visitors every year?

How long has your town been around?

How many people live in your town?

What are some popular places to go in your town?

Is there a food your town is known for?

DATE / TIME ::

LOCATION ::

SUBJECT ::

DATE / TIME ::

LOCATION ::

SUBJECT ::

DATE / TIME ::

LOCATION ::

SUBJECT ::

SUPPORT SYSTEMS

You'll take on many challenging missions and tasks at Explorer Academy, some that will test your bravery and strength. To get through them, explorers rely on their friends, family, and teachers. For example, Cruz gets help from his personal support team: his dad, his aunt Marisol, his best friend Lani, and his new friends on Team Cousteau. Who are the members of your personal support team? How have they helped you out during tough times?

DATE / TIME ::

LOCATION ::

SUBJECT ::

DATE / TIME ::

LOCATION ::

SUBJECT ::

CREATE YOUR OWN CODE

Learning codes and ciphers is crucial to keeping mission information classified. At Explorer Academy, you'll learn how to decipher codes, as well as how to create some of your own.

Your task, recruit: Create your own substitution cipher. A substitution cipher is a type of code that uses symbols to replace letters of the alphabet, such as A = +, B = ^, etc. Come up with your own cipher by drawing a unique symbol in the box below each letter. Copy the code and give it to a friend so you can exchange secret messages.

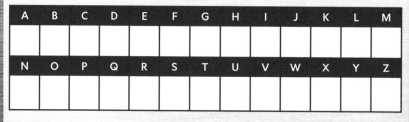

A	B	C	D	E	F	G	H	I	J	K	L	M

N	O	P	Q	R	S	T	U	V	W	X	Y	Z

USE YOUR CODE TO WRITE OUT THE MOTTO OF EXPLORER ACADEMY:
TO DISCOVER. TO INNOVATE. TO PROTECT.

DATE / TIME ::   LOCATION ::

SUBJECT ::

DATE / TIME ::   LOCATION ::

SUBJECT ::

AFRICAN SAFARI

Ready for your next destination? Your explorer team is headed to a savanna in southern Africa to design a wildlife conservation program. What five animals do you hope you'll encounter there? Big cats such as lions and cheetahs? Fast runners such as gazelles? Majestic African elephants? There are so many to choose from!

DATE / TIME ::   LOCATION ::

SUBJECT ::

CIPHER SCAVENGER HUNT

Before she mysteriously died, Petra Coronado was working on a top secret scientific formula that could change the course of the world as we know it. She left cipher pieces all over the globe for her son, Cruz, to find and use to track down the missing formula. Knowing Nebula agents would be hot on Cruz's trail to get to the pieces first, Petra carefully chose where she hid them.

Plan out where you would hide your own secret cipher pieces for a trusted friend or family member in eight locations around the world. Pinpoint and label the locations you select on the map, and on the following page, write about why you hid them in the places you chose.

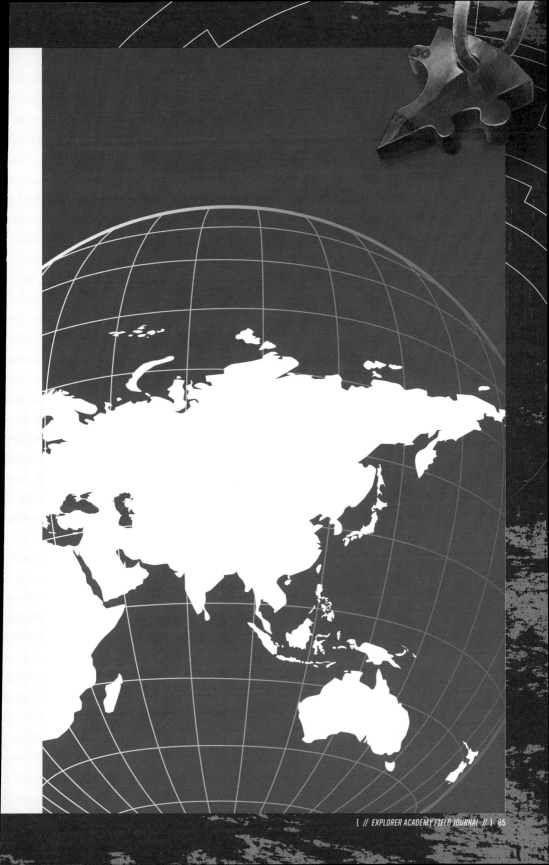

Write about why you hid the cipher pieces in the places you chose.

PIECE ONE

PIECE TWO

PIECE THREE

PIECE FOUR

PIECE FIVE

PIECE SIX

PIECE SEVEN

PIECE EIGHT

DATE / TIME ::   LOCATION ::

SUBJECT ::

WHAT'S COOKING?

How adventurous is your appetite? On every mission, recruits get the chance to taste the local cuisine—everything from sushi in Tokyo to couscous in Morocco. What are five foods that you've never eaten before but would love to try?

1
2
3
4
5

DATE / TIME ::

LOCATION ::

SUBJECT ::

MARINA ELLIOTT

Marina Elliott
Biological anthropologist

Biological anthropologist Marina Elliott descends deep into caves, often crawling through tight passages and sliding down chutes in order to find and investigate human remains hidden deep beneath Earth's surface.

This important work can be dangerous and difficult, but she doesn't have to undertake it alone: "I have an amazing team of cavers and excavators that I work with and they are some of the most professional, capable, and awesome people in the world. The knowledge and the trust we have in each other's skills and judgment make a big difference in overcoming whatever obstacles we face." Marina says that the strong communication skills and sense of trust that she has with her team is necessary to complete a mission. "We literally put our lives in each other's hands each time we go into the field."

It's always best to foster and maintain close relationships with your teammates, just like Cruz does with his friends on Team Cousteau. The adventures you'll have with your team won't only build your bonds with one another, they will impact you as an individual: "Exploring is all about learning something new, and that can be scary sometimes, but prepare yourself as best you can and then go for it—you may just discover something no one else has known before, and you will certainly learn something about yourself!"

What makes you a good member of a team?

Marina on a caving expedition

DATE / TIME ::

LOCATION ::

SUBJECT ::

DATE / TIME ::

LOCATION ::

SUBJECT ::

Students at the Academy have the important task of studying weather patterns to learn about the health of the planet. Even small changes in temperatures year after year around the world can indicate a human-made problem in the environment.

WEATHER WATCHER

MISSION 4.0

YOUR MISSION, RECRUIT: Use this page to keep track of the weather where you live. If any of these weather events happen, record the date and any observations you make during the event.

MISSION 1.0 | MISSION 2.0 | MISSION 3.0 | **MISSION 4.0** | MISSION 5.0

Temperature above 100°F (38°C):

Temperature below 32°F (0°C):

Hail:

Sleet:

Heavy rain:

Thunder:

Lightning:

Hurricane or high winds:

Snow or blizzard:

Tornado:

DATE / TIME ::

LOCATION ::

SUBJECT ::

DATE / TIME ::

LOCATION ::

SUBJECT ::

DATE / TIME ::

LOCATION ::

SUBJECT ::

What do you think
Cruz is thinking about?

QUALITIES THAT COUNT

Dr. Regina Hightower, president of Explorer Academy, chooses recruits who are curious, enthusiastic, and dedicated. Which of these qualities do you have? What other qualities do you have that make you an asset to the Academy?

DATE / TIME ::

LOCATION ::

SUBJECT ::

MAKE A MASCOT

Hubbard the West Highland white terrier is the unofficial mascot of Explorer Academy. What kind of pet would be a good companion for your exploration team? Draw it here and give it a name.

DATE / TIME ::

LOCATION ::

SUBJECT ::

DATE / TIME ::   LOCATION ::

SUBJECT ::

TEAM CONNECTION

Cruz and Bryndis both love to surf. Sailor and Emmett both like to tackle problems. Which member of Team Cousteau are you most like, and why? Everyone is unique and special in their own way—write about why you're different than them, too!

DATE / TIME ::   **LOCATION ::**

SUBJECT ::

DATE / TIME ::

LOCATION ::

SUBJECT ::

DATE / TIME ::   LOCATION ::

SUBJECT ::

Some Explorer Academy students have gone on to explore the ultimate frontier: outer space! Until you graduate, you can explore the galaxies without leaving Earth.

STARGAZING

MISSION 5.0

YOUR MISSION, RECRUIT: Spend one week looking at the night sky and record what you see. Is it clear or cloudy? Can you see the moon? If so, what shape is it? Do you see any stars or constellations that you recognize? Any unusual lights, such as shooting stars or comets? Write down what you observe.

mission 1.0 | mission 2.0 | mission 3.0 | mission 4.0 | **mission 5.0**

NIGHT 1:

NIGHT 2:

NIGHT 3:

NIGHT 4:

NIGHT 5:

NIGHT 6:

NIGHT 7:

DATE / TIME ::   LOCATION ::

SUBJECT ::

BRIAN SKERRY

Brian Skerry
Explorer & photographer

Brian Skerry, an underwater photographer and National Geographic explorer who regularly dives next to massive whales and sharks, knows that out in the field, you have to "expect the unexpected." It's during these unpredictable moments that an explorer's physical and mental strength are put to the test.

Skerry recognizes that no matter how much planning and preparation you do, all explorers run into roadblocks during their expeditions. But "overcoming problems will ultimately determine your success. An explorer should have a realistic understanding of this before beginning any project and recognize that, inevitably, things you do not plan for will happen." One of the most important tricks Skerry has learned is to "give [himself] time to think things through and [not] make snap decisions." He finds that oftentimes, like Cruz brainstorming with Team Cousteau, talking about an issue with expedition team members results in a solution.

Other times, when the stress of a situation seems too overwhelming, Skerry will take a moment to "clear [his] head by doing something that takes [him] away mentally from the given situation," like watching a movie on his computer or reading a book. The process of decompressing from a day's events is all about reflection, and helps him to avoid being consumed by the project: "It reminds me that there are other important things in life and often gives me perspective on the problem at hand."

What is one thing you do to relieve stress when things get tough?

DATE / TIME ::

LOCATION ::

SUBJECT ::

TEAM LOGO

Design a logo for your team of
Explorer Academy recruits.

EA

STEP ONE: SKETCH ALL YOUR IDEAS FIRST.

STEP TWO: SIMPLIFY YOUR CONCEPTS INTO ONE EASY-TO-READ LOGO WITH TEXT AND/OR DRAWINGS.

STEP THREE: REDRAW YOUR FINAL LOGO HERE. ADD COLOR IF YOU LIKE.

THE EXPLORER'S APPRENTICE

Each team of recruits is named after a famous explorer:
Ferdinand Magellan, Amelia Earhart, Jacques Cousteau, and
Galileo Galilei. Imagine that you could go back in time and be
the student of one of these explorers. Where would you go,
and what mission would you take on together?

FERDINAND
MAGELLAN

AMELIA
EARHART

JACQUES
COUSTEAU

GALILEO
GALILEI

DATE / TIME ::

LOCATION ::

SUBJECT ::

DATE / TIME ::

LOCATION ::

SUBJECT ::

GOODBYE FOR NOW!

DEAR EXPLORER,

Great job, recruit! You really put a lot of effort and detail into this field journal. I can speak for everyone at Explorer Academy when I say that we hope you have learned a little bit more about yourself—what makes you special, and what you are passionate about exploring.

Even though you've successfully completed the missions and prompts in this journal as part of your training, don't feel like you have to stop undertaking expeditions and writing! Keeping a journal is a great way to navigate your own thoughts and feelings as you go through life. I encourage you to keep track of your observations of the world around you. After all, the best explorers are those who take time to reflect on what they've done and what they've learned along the way.

So keep writing, recruit, and always remember: Discover. Innovate. Protect.

TARYN SECLIFF
DORM ADVISER

Since 1888, the National Geographic Society has funded more than 12,000 research, exploration, and preservation projects around the world. The Society receives funds from National Geographic Partners, LLC, funded in part by your purchase. A portion of the proceeds from this book supports this vital work. To learn more, visit natgeo.com/info.

For more information, visit nationalgeographic.com, call 1-877-873-6846, or write to the following address:

National Geographic Partners
1145 17th Street N.W.
Washington, D.C. 20036-4688 U.S.A.

Visit us online at nationalgeographic.com/books

For librarians and teachers: nationalgeographic.com/books/librarians-and-educators

More for kids from National Geographic: natgeokids.com

National Geographic Kids magazine inspires children to explore their world with fun yet educational articles on animals, science, nature, and more. Using fresh storytelling and amazing photography, *Nat Geo Kids* shows kids ages 6 to 14 the fascinating truth about the world—and why they should care.
kids.nationalgeographic.com/subscribe

For rights or permissions inquiries, please contact National Geographic Books Subsidiary Rights: bookrights@natgeo.com

PHOTO CREDITS
All artwork by Scott Plumbe unless otherwise noted below.
NGIC=National Geographic Image Collection; SS=Shutterstock
Cover (silver porthole), Ase/SS; cover (brass cipher dial), Eileen Tweedy/SS; cover (water in porthole), Willyam Bradberry/SS; cover (topo map background texture), DamienGeso/SS; spine (dark clouds layer in porthole), elegeyda/SS; various (watercolor texture), white snow/SS; various (metallic background texture), Shubin Vitaliy/SS; various (red metal background), Eky Studio/SS; various (red honeycomb background), Marta Ortiz/SS; various (blue metal background), tsingha25/SS; various (blue glass background), Igor Marusichenko/SS; various (blue shiny paint background), PixieMe/SS; various (blue grid background), Eky Studio/SS; various (blue elevator background), chinasong/SS; various (blue architectural background), Vladitto/SS; various (orange porthole burst), Igor Zh./SS; various (black-and-white grunge texture), MiAdS/SS; various (blue circular techy lines layer), Titima Ongkantong/SS; various (blue grid pattern layer), Edgieus/SS; 3, Michal Vitek/SS; 10, Ondrej Prosicky/SS; 20-21, Africa Studio/SS; 30, Amy Johansson/SS; 35, Leksele/SS; 38-39 (open journal), magicinfoto/SS; 38 (compass), Irochka/Dreamstime; 38 (torn paper), FabrikaSimf/SS; 38 (portrait), Mike Parmalee/NGIC; 39, Barry Brown/NGIC; 46, Steve Collender/SS; 48-49 (open journal), magicinfoto/SS; 48 (compass), Irochka/Dreamstime; 48 (torn paper), FabrikaSimf/SS; 48 (portrait), Kat Keene Hogue/NGIC; 49, Alex Staroseltsev/SS; 60, Kosmos111/Dreamstime; 80, Bildagentur Zoona/SS; 81 (lion cub), Eric Isselee/SS; 81 (elephant), Susan Schmitz/SS; 84-85, rzymuR/SS; 90 (UP), CLM/SS; 90 (LO), picturepartners/SS; 94-95 (open journal), magicinfoto/SS; 94 (compass), Irochka/Dreamstime; 94 (torn paper), FabrikaSimf/SS; 94 (portrait), Robert Clark/NGIC; 95 (ropes), swinner/SS; 95 (caving expedition), Robert Clark/NGIC; 100, John D Sirlin/SS; 109 (starry sky layer), Ase/SS; 126 (dark starry night layer in porthole), Tjefferson/SS; 130-131 (open journal), magicinfoto/SS; 130 (compass), Irochka/Dreamstime; 130 (torn paper), FabrikaSimf/SS; 130 (portrait), Brain J. Skerry/NGIC; 131 (water droplets layer), Macrovector/SS; 136 (Ferdinand Magellan), Library of Congress Prints and Photographs Division; 136 (Amelia Earhart), Library of Congress Prints and Photographs Division; 137 (Jacques Cousteau), AP Photo; 137 (Galileo Galilei), Georgios Kollidas/SS

Designed by Rachael Hamm Plett, Moduza Design

Trade Paperback ISBN: 978-1-4263-3684-3

The publisher would like to acknowledge the following people for making this journal possible: Tracey West, author; Avery Naughton, project editor; Lori Epstein, director of photography; Eva Absher-Schantz, vice president of visual identity; Alix Inchausti, production editor; and Anne LeongSon and Gus Tello, design production assistants.

Printed in Hong Kong
20/PPHK/1